Dear Parent:

Buckle up! You are about to join your child on a very exciting journey. The destination? Independent reading!

Road to Reading will help you and your child get there. The program offers books at five levels, or Miles, that accompany children from their first attempts at reading to successfully reading on their own. Each Mile is paved with engaging stories and delightful artwork.

Getting Started
For children who know the alphabet and are eager to begin reading
- easy words • fun rhythms • big type • picture clues

Reading With Help
For children who recognize some words and sound out others with help
- short sentences • pattern stories • simple plotlines

Reading On Your Own
For children who are ready to read easy stories by themselves
- longer sentences • more complex plotlines • easy dialogue

First Chapter Books
For children who want to take the plunge into chapter books
- bite-size chapters • short paragraphs • full-color art

Chapter Books
For children who are comfortable reading independently
- longer chapters • occasional black-and-white illustrations

There's no need to hurry through the Miles. Road to Reading is designed without age or grade levels. Children can progress at their own speed, developing confidence and pride in their reading ability no matter what their age or grade.

So sit back and enjoy the ride—every Mile of the way!

A GOLDEN BOOK • New York
Golden Books Publishing Company, Inc. New York, New York 10106

ISBN: 0-307-26339-8

10 9 8 7 6 5 4 3 2 1

Grace
on the Ice

Peggy Fleming • Dorothy Hamill
Michelle Kwan

by Abigail Tabby
illustrated with photographs

Ice skaters make
their sport look easy.
They smile as they
leap, spin, and glide
across the rink.
But ice skating is tough.
Imagine trying to twirl
in the air and land on a
thin metal blade—
on the ice!

Skating is hard enough
in a quiet practice rink.
Now imagine there are thousands,
or even millions, of people watching!
The pressure is intense.
Each skater wants to do her best
for her coach, her country, and herself.

This book tells the story
of three amazing athletes
who overcame the pressure—
and showed the world
grace on the ice.

Peggy Fleming

Peggy Fleming is known as
one of the most graceful skaters
in the history of the sport.
Even before she went
to the Olympic Winter Games,
people were talking about her.
"Have you seen how beautifully
she skates?" they'd say.
"She's like a ballerina on ice."

Peggy was an excellent skater.
But there was a lot of
pressure on her.
In 1961, Peggy was eleven years old.
She was home training when
the entire U.S. figure skating team
was killed in a terrible plane crash.
With all the top skaters gone,
it was up to the young skaters
to build a winning team.

Young Peggy feels the pressure

Peggy trained hard.

She made it a habit to practice

her whole routine, even if she fell.

Most skaters would stop and start over.

But not Peggy.

She wanted to learn to concentrate.

All her hard work paid off.

In 1964, at the national championships,

Peggy surprised everyone

by taking first place.

Suddenly, all eyes were on Peggy.
Everyone was watching her train
for the 1968 Olympic Winter Games
in Grenoble, France.
All the newspapers were saying
that she was going to win.

These Olympic Winter Games
would be the first ones
shown live and in color on TV.
The whole world would be watching.
Peggy was worried.
What if she lost?
She would let her country down.

The night before Peggy's performance at
the Olympic Winter Games

Halfway through the competition,

Peggy was in first place

with a huge lead.

Then it was time for her last routine.

Peggy glided onto the ice.

The music started and

Peggy began to skate.

But things did not go as planned.

First, Peggy did a single jump

instead of a double.

Then she stumbled on her

next jump—a double lutz.

Peggy knew the judges would
take off points for these mistakes.
But Peggy didn't quit.
Just as she did in practice,
Peggy finished the program.
She skated the rest of
her routine perfectly!

The judges gave Peggy the
highest marks of all the skaters.
She brought home the United States'
only gold medal from the 1968 Games!
Peggy Fleming was a star.

Dorothy Hamill

Dorothy's dream comes true

Dorothy Hamill started skating

on a frozen pond near her house

when she was eight years old.

She loved skating,

and begged her mother for lessons.

Soon Dorothy was skating every day.

Her mother drove her to the skating rink

at four o'clock in the morning

so she could practice before school.

After school, while her friends played,

Dorothy headed back to the rink.

But Dorothy didn't mind.

Her dream was to skate

in the Olympic Winter Games.

Dorothy wasn't quite

as graceful as Peggy.

But Dorothy had powerful jumps.

She also had fantastic spins,

like the Hamill-Camel,

which was named for her.

And Dorothy had charm.

Girls all over the world

copied her trademark short haircut.

No one could get enough of her.

At Dorothy's first big international
competition in France,
she was chosen to skate thirteenth.
Would it be bad luck?
Dorothy was worried.
Her coach told her that in Europe,
thirteen is actually a *lucky* number.
He gave her a charm with
the number thirteen.
Dorothy wore the charm
around her neck—
and won the competition!
After that, she wore the charm
whenever she skated.

Dorothy at the U.S. National Figure
Skating Championships

A few years later, the number thirteen

was lucky for Dorothy again.

In the 1976 Olympic Winter Games

in Innsbruck, Austria,

she skated on February 13.

During her performance,

she landed a perfect double axel.

Dorothy had skated better than ever.

Before the scores were shown,

the television announcer yelled,

"She's done it! She's won the gold!"

And she had!

The next day—Valentine's Day—

the newspapers crowned Dorothy

America's sweetheart.

After the Olympic Winter Games,
many skaters retire.
Dorothy wanted to keep competing.
She wanted to skate in the
world championships in Sweden.
People told her she was crazy.
She had already won a gold medal.
Why not stop while she was ahead?
But Dorothy was determined to show
the world that she could win again.

Nobody seemed to think she could do it.

As the competition grew closer,

Dorothy began to feel the pressure.

Maybe she should have retired after all.

But just as she always did in the past,

Dorothy pulled through and won.

Even after winning
the world championships,
Dorothy kept skating.
Today she is one of the
oldest skaters still performing.
She trains up to six hours a day
to stay in top shape.
When people ask Dorothy when
she will stop skating, she laughs.
"Never!" she says.

Michelle Kwan

Michelle skates at the
U.S. Olympic Festival

Michelle Kwan's skating career
began when she was five years old.
By the time she was twelve,
Michelle was training at a rink
a few hours from her home.
Her father and sister lived with her,
and her mother and brother
visited on weekends.

It was hard for the family.
Michelle's father often asked
if she was sure she wanted to put
all that work into skating.
Michelle always said yes.

Michelle's grace reminded people
of Peggy Fleming.
She was also a strong jumper
like Dorothy Hamill.
Michelle had it all, and soon she started
winning junior competitions.

Michelle with her choreographer

Michelle wanted to move up
to the senior level.
Her coach told her to wait.
"There is plenty of time," he said.
But Michelle felt ready.

While her coach was away,

Michelle secretly took the test

to move up to the senior level.

She passed!

Michelle was happy.

Her coach was not.

"You'll have to train harder now,"

he told her.

"You'll be competing against girls

who are older and stronger than you."

Michelle shows off her gold medal at the
World Figure Skating Championships

Michelle was up for the challenge.

She trained so much,

she sometimes had to be

dragged off the ice!

"Just one more time!"

she would cry,

trying to make each jump perfect.

Her hard work paid off.

She won nearly every

competition she entered.

Michelle falls during a performance

But then there was trouble.

Michelle began to fall in competitions.

She had injured her foot,

and when she did jumps

she was often in pain.

She had also grown taller,

and it was hard for her to get

used to her new body.

At the 1998 national championships,

Michelle had a lot to prove.

If she did not skate well,

people would think

her career was over.

Michelle is usually nervous
before a competition.
She tells herself, "I want to win."
That night, she told herself
she just wanted to skate well.
And she did better than that!
In her two routines,
Michelle received fifteen perfect marks!
It was the most ever given to any skater
at the national championships.

That same year, Michelle went on
to win a silver medal at the
1998 Olympic Winter Games in Japan.
Many people were surprised that
Michelle did not win the gold.
But Michelle was thrilled.
She said she was the happiest
silver medalist ever!
Michelle's terrific attitude
made people admire her even more.
Skating fans in America
and around the world are rooting
for her to win the gold at the
2002 Olympic Winter Games
in Salt Lake City, Utah.

Peggy Fleming, Dorothy Hamill,
and Michelle Kwan all proved
they are graceful on the ice.
They are graceful off the ice, too—
and that's what makes them
true champions.